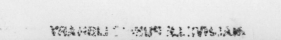

BOB AND OTTO

Robert O. Bruel

Pictures by

Nick Bruel

A NEAL PORTER BOOK
ROARING BROOK PRESS
NEW MILFORD, CONNECTICUT

For Mary, aka: Yusing, aka: Mom, aka: Wiffy

Text copyright © 2007 by Mary Yusing Bruel

Illustrations copyright © 2007 by Nick Bruel

A Neal Porter Book

Published by Roaring Brook Press

Roaring Brook Press is a division of Holtzbrinck Publishing Holdings Limited Partnership

143 West Street, New Milford, Connecticut 06776

Distributed in Canada by H. B. Fenn and Company Ltd.

Library of Congress Cataloging-in-Publication Data

Bruel, Nick.

Bob and Otto / by Nick Bruel and Robert O. Bruel. — 1st ed.

p. cm.

"A Neal Porter Book."

Summary: Otto the worm is shocked to discover that his best friend Bob is actually a caterpillar who emerges one day as a butterfly.

ISBN-13: 978-1-59643-203-1   ISBN-10: 1-59643-203-9

[1. Worms—Fiction. 2. Caterpillars—Fiction. 3. Friendship—Fiction.]   I. Bruel, Robert O.   II. Title.

PZ7.B82832Bl 2007   [E]—dc22   2006012008

Roaring Brook Press books are available for special promotions and premiums.

For details contact: Director of Special Markets, Holtzbrinck Publishers.

First Edition April 2007

Book design by Jennifer Browne

Printed in China

10 9 8 7 6 5 4 3 2 1

Once, there were two very good friends.

It was spring, and everything was lively
and exciting.

These two very good friends spent each day
digging in the ground, playing in the grass,
and eating the leaves that fell
from the old tree.

But one day...

Bob
looked
up.

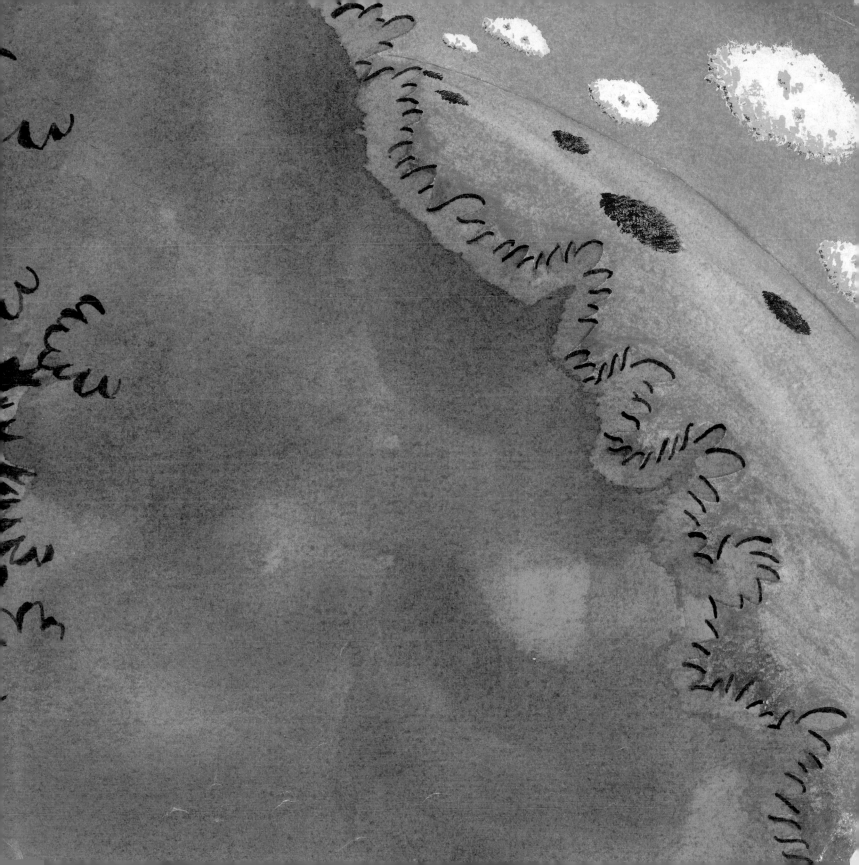

"I need to climb this tree," he said. "I want to see how the world looks from up there."

"Up there?!" said Otto.
"But it's so nice down here.
When it's hot and dry, you can
dig deep into the ground where
it's cool and damp. And when
it rains, you can come
back up! Life is good
just where we are.
Why would you want
to go up there?"

"Because it's important," said Bob.
And up the tree he went.

"It's important down here, too," said Otto. And down into the ground he went.

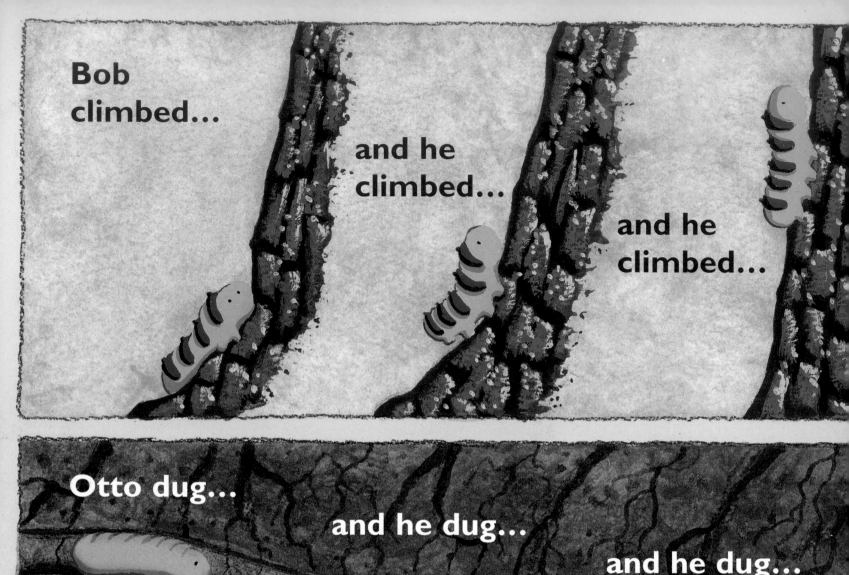

and he ate...

and he ate...

until he felt quite sleepy.

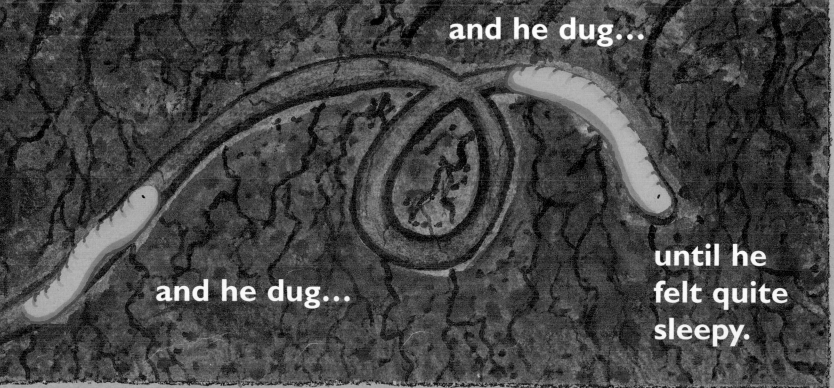

and he dug...

and he dug...

until he felt quite sleepy.

So Bob slept...

and he slept...

and he slept...

But Otto still dug...

and he dug...

and he dug...

and he slept...

for many, many days and nights.

and he dug...

and dug some more.

When Bob woke up, he was so full of joy, he felt like flying!

So he flew...

Otto loved digging so much...

he dug...

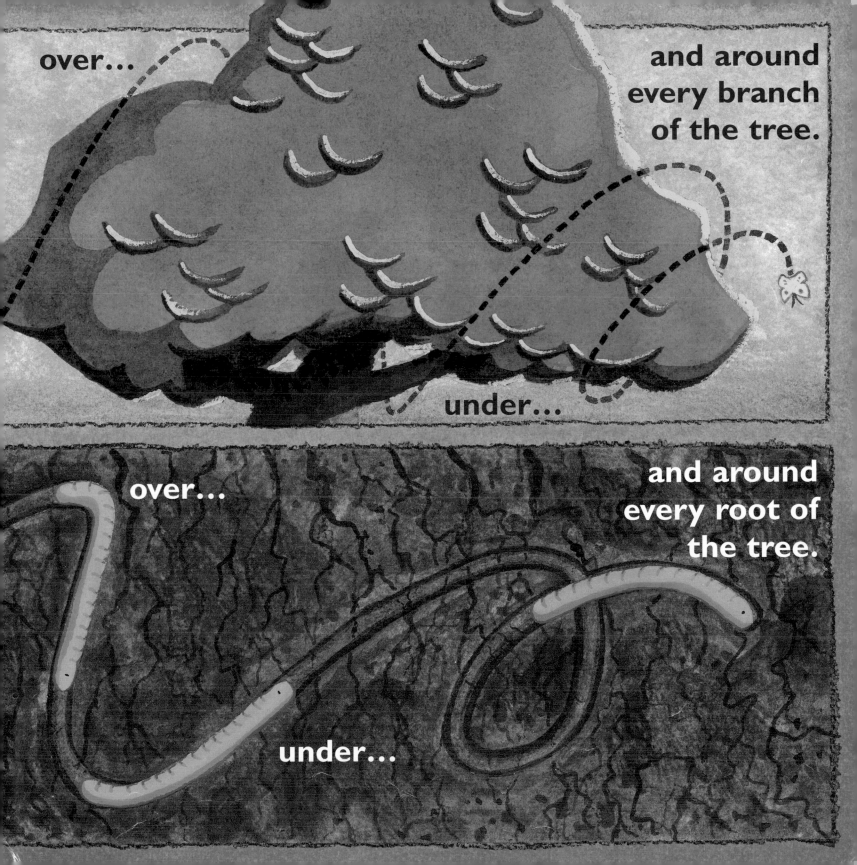

"Because," said Otto, "if I had climbed up the old tree with you when you asked me to, then maybe I would have grown big, beautiful wings like yours! And maybe I could fly."

BUT I DIDN'T.

"While you were digging...all I did was eat.

"While you were digging...all I did was sleep.

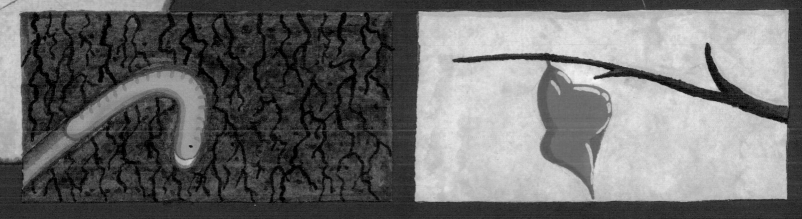

"While you were digging...all I did was fly around.

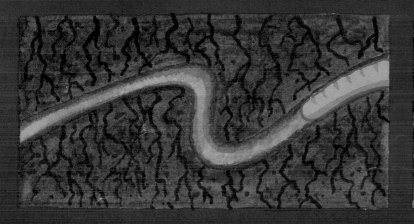

"But while you were digging,
you loosened the soil...

so the roots could drink water,

so the tree could grow tall,

so the leaves would be green,

so I could eat the leaves...

And friends
are important.